The Pug Who Wanted to Be a Mermaid

The Pug

Who Wanted to Be a

Mermaid

by Bella Swift

ALADDIN   New York   London   Toronto   Sydney   New Delhi

Text by Anne Marie Ryan

Illustrations by Nina Jones and Artful Doodlers

ALADDIN

An imprint of Simon & Schuster Children's Publishing Division
1230 Avenue of the Americas, New York, New York 10020
First Aladdin paperback edition April 2022
Text copyright © 2021 by Orchard Books
Illustrations copyright © 2021 by Orchard Books
Originally published in Great Britain in 2021 by the Watts Publishing Group
Also available in an Aladdin hardcover edition.
All rights reserved, including the right of reproduction in whole or in part in any form.
ALADDIN and related logo are registered trademarks of Simon & Schuster, Inc.
For information about special discounts for bulk purchases, please contact Simon & Schuster Special Sales at 1-866-506-1949 or business@simonandschuster.com.
The Simon & Schuster Speakers Bureau can bring authors to your live event.
For more information or to book an event contact the Simon & Schuster Speakers Bureau at 1-866-248-3049 or visit our website at www.simonspeakers.com.
The text of this book was set in Bembo Std.
Manufactured in the United States of America 0322 OFF
2 4 6 8 10 9 7 5 3 1
Library of Congress Control Number 2021933725
ISBN 9781534486881 (hc)
ISBN 9781534486874 (pbk)
ISBN 9781534486898 (ebook)

Contents

Chapter One

Peggy the pug was flopped under the big oak tree in the back garden, panting in the shade. It was *soooo* hot! On summer days like today, she wished her short, tan-colored fur wasn't quite so warm and cozy. A fly buzzed around her nose, but Peggy couldn't be bothered to swat it away with her paw. She lolled on the grass and thought about cold things, like the kitchen floor tiles . . . snow . . . and ICE CREAM!

"Peggy!" someone called from the house, interrupting her vanilla-flavored daydream.

Hearing her friend Chloe's voice, Peggy sat up and wagged her curly little tail. She always had energy to play with her best friend!

Chloe and her little sister, Ruby, came running over, flushed and sweaty.

"Guess what!" said Chloe, crouching down to stroke Peggy. "School's out! It's the summer holidays!"

"No more homework until September!" sang Ruby, doing a cartwheel on the grass.

"Yippee!" barked Peggy excitedly. She would see more of Chloe and Ruby—and their big brother, Finn—over the summer holidays. She missed the kids when they were at school.

Dad came out, holding a big black poster board with brightly colored balls of different sizes glued to it. "How was your last day of school?" he asked the girls.

"Fun!" said Ruby. "We got extra play-time, and I got a certificate for being a Super Helper."

"Well done," said Dad. "By the way, what is this thing? I found it in the kitchen."

"Oh, that's my solar system project," said Chloe. "I made it in science class this term. My teacher said I could take it home."

"Oh," said Dad. "It's . . . very big."

"Not compared to a planet," said Chloe. "Did you know that Neptune is four times the size of Earth?"

"Is that so?" said Dad. "Well, this was certainly taking up most of the kitchen table."

"I'll keep it in my bedroom," said Chloe, taking her solar system from Dad. "Is it okay if I go to the park? Everyone from school is meeting up there."

"Can I come too?" pleaded Ruby.

"And me!" said Peggy, but to the humans it just sounded like barking.

"Sure," said Dad. "Finn just texted to say he's hanging out at the park with some friends. I'll ask him to keep an eye on you."

Chloe took her solar system project up to her bedroom. Then she packed a bag with some snacks and clipped on Peggy's lead, and they headed to the park. The sidewalk felt hot against Peggy's paws as she trotted along by Chloe's side.

"Look! There's Finn!" said Ruby as they went through the park gates. She waved to her big brother, who was kicking a soccer

ball around on the grass with his friend
Zach. Peggy tried to chase after the soccer
ball, but Chloe tugged on her lead. "This
way, Peggy. I'm meeting Ellie and Hannah."

Ruby spotted some of her friends from
her kindergarten class on the playground
and ran over to join them on the merry-
go-round. Just looking at them spinning
around made Peggy feel dizzy!

Chloe's friends were sitting on the grass

near the playground, making daisy chains. Peggy was delighted to see that Hannah had brought her little terrier, Princess, along.

"Hi, Peggy!" yapped Princess. She had a yellow bow in her fur that matched Hannah's sundress perfectly.

As the two little dogs sniffed each other happily, Chloe sat down with her friends.

"I'm so glad it's the summer holidays," said Hannah, putting her daisy chain around Princess's neck.

"Me too," said Ellie. "My family's going camping for two weeks. We're sleeping in a tent and hiking every day. At night, we're going to roast marshmallows on the campfire."

"That sounds fun," said Hannah, fanning herself with her sun hat. "I'm going on holiday to Spain. We're staying in a hotel that has two pools—one of them even has a water slide."

"Oooh!" said Chloe. "That's so cool." She frowned. "But what about Princess? Can she go on the plane with you?"

"Princess is going to stay in a kennel while we're away," said Hannah, stroking her dog's head. "She really loves it there, with all the other dogs. It's just like a holiday for her, too."

Princess groaned and rolled her eyes. "I hate it at that kennel," she told Peggy. "It's awful. I have to sleep in a cage, and all the other dogs are constantly barking."

Peggy felt sorry for her friend. A kennel sounded a lot like a dog shelter. She had been in one of those before Chloe and her family had adopted her. She'd never felt so scared and lonely before.

"At least it's only for a bit," Peggy said, trying to reassure her. "You know Hannah will come back for you."

"Where are you going on holiday, Chloe?" asked Hannah.

Chloe shrugged. "I don't think we're

going anywhere this year. My mum's been so busy setting up her café."

Chloe's mum ran a café called Pups and Cups, where people could bring their dogs and buy tasty treats—for dogs and humans.

"That's too bad," said Ellie. "But at least you always get lots of yummy snacks from the café."

"True . . . ," said Chloe, reaching into her bag and taking out a plastic container of chocolate chip cookies that she shared with her friends.

"Hey," yapped Princess. "What about us?"

Peggy whined
hopefully, and
Chloe took
out another
container. She
gave Peggy and
Princess each a

bacon-and-peanut-butter-flavored dog
biscuit shaped like a bone.

They stayed in the park until the sun
began to set, and then Finn rounded up
his sisters.

"Tomorrow I'm going to sleep late,"
he said, bouncing his soccer ball up and
down as they walked home.

Sleeping late sounded good to Peggy. She was exhausted after playing with Princess.

As they came up the front path, Mum was just getting home from the café. "Hi," she said. "I ordered pizza. It's too hot to cook today."

When the pizzas arrived, Peggy's family sat down at the table and tucked into their dinner.

"I love pizza!" said Ruby, biting into a slice and getting tomato sauce all over her face.

"Zach is going on holiday to Italy with his parents," said Finn. "I bet he'll eat pizza every single day."

"I wish we were going on holiday," said Chloe, sighing as she picked a mushroom off her slice of pizza.

Mum and Dad exchanged looks. "Actually," said Mum, grinning, "we have some good news. The café's been doing pretty well, so we're going to the seaside for a week."

The children stared at their parents in disbelief.

"No way!" shouted Finn. Chloe and Ruby shrieked with excitement. It was so loud that Peggy had to cover her ears with her paws!

"We're staying in a place called Mermaid

Cottage," said Dad, showing them a picture on his phone. "It has three bedrooms and it's right by the beach."

Chloe's eyes widened as she looked at the screen. "It's so cute," she said.

"I can't wait for a break," said Mum. "I'm going to lie on the beach and read in the sunshine."

"Not me," said Ruby. "I'm going to build sandcastles."

"Do you think we could go deep-sea fishing?" asked Finn.

Dad nodded. "Definitely."

"I'm going to go swimming every day," said Chloe. Then she added, "And maybe I'll even get to see a mermaid."

Everyone was excited about the holiday—except Peggy. Would she have to stay in a dog kennel like Princess?

"Wait a minute," said Chloe, as if she'd read Peggy's mind. "Who will look after Peggy?"

"We will," said Mum. "She's coming with us, of course."

"Did you hear that, Pegs?" asked Chloe, scooping Peggy onto her lap. "You're going on holiday!"

Peggy gave a bark of joy and wagged her tail. She'd never been to the seaside before, and she couldn't wait!

Chapter Two

"Just one more sleep until we go on holiday!" announced Chloe, marking an X on the kitchen calendar. The children had been busy for the first few weeks of the summer holidays. Finn had gone to music camp, Chloe had had tennis lessons with her friends, and Ruby had taken a swimming class at the local recreation center. She'd just come back from the pool, and her curly hair was still damp.

"I swam underwater today," Ruby said proudly. "My teacher called me a little mermaid."

"Ooh! *The Little Mermaid*," said Chloe. "Let's watch it again."

The girls helped themselves to fruity Popcicles from the freezer, then went into the living room and switched on the television. Peggy sat between them and watched the film too. She liked it because there were lots of funny sea creatures in it, like crabs and seagulls.

I wonder if I'll make any new animal friends on holiday, she thought hopefully.

When their favorite song came on, the girls jumped off the sofa and started dancing around the living room.

"Under the sea!" sang Chloe, twirling her sister around.

"Under the sea!" chorused Ruby.

They knew all the words. So did Peggy. She joined in, howling along to the music.

When the film was over, Finn came in. "I can't believe you watched that stupid old movie again," he said. "You've seen it a million times already."

"We might see a mermaid on holiday," Ruby told Finn.

"Yeah right," he scoffed. "Mermaids aren't real."

Chloe stuck her tongue out at her

brother. "Just because you've never seen one doesn't mean they don't exist."

"Let's watch something decent," Finn said, grabbing the remote. Chloe tried to get it from him, but he held it up over her head and switched to a documentary about sharks.

"Awesome," said Finn as an enormous great white shark swam across the screen, its jaws open to reveal rows of sharp teeth. "Maybe we'll see one of these on holiday."

Peggy whimpered and covered her eyes with her paws as the shark attacked a school of fish.

"Maybe one will eat you," said Chloe grumpily.

Ruby's eyes widened in fear. "Are there really sharks at the seaside?"

"Don't worry, Rubes," said Finn, tousling her hair. "There aren't any great whites where we're going. Just little sharks."

That didn't make Peggy feel very reassured. She was only little—even a small shark could probably eat her in one bite!

Everyone was too excited to eat much breakfast the next morning, even though Dad had cooked bacon and eggs to use up what was left in the fridge.

"I can't believe we're going on holiday today!" Chloe said, scraping her leftover breakfast into Peggy's bowl.

"We've got lots to do before we leave," said Mum, handing everyone a packing list.

"I'd better get Coco's things together," said Chloe. "Ellie's coming to collect her soon."

Chloe's friend Ellie was looking after Coco the bunny while the rest of the family was at the seaside. Peggy followed Chloe outside to the back garden. As Chloe got a bag of wood shavings, a travel carrier, and some rabbit food out of the shed, Peggy went over to the rabbit hutch to chat with Coco.

"Hi, Peggy," said the black-and-white rabbit. "Are you excited about your holiday? I bet you'll have lots of fun."

Peggy nodded. "I'm sorry you can't come with us, though."

"Don't worry," said Coco, her whiskers twitching. "I can't wait to see my mum again. We've got so much to catch up on. It will be great."

Coco's mum was Daisy, Ellie's pet rabbit. Peggy was relieved to hear that Coco was looking forward to her holiday, too!

When Ellie arrived, Chloe took Coco out of her hutch and gave her one last cuddle. Then she put the bunny into the travel carrier.

"I'll take really good care of her," promised Ellie.

"I know you will," said Chloe, smiling.

"Send me some pics," said Ellie.

"I will," said Chloe.

"Have fun with Daisy!" Peggy barked.

Once Ellie had taken Coco home, Chloe went upstairs to start packing. She

opened her chest of drawers and started

taking out shorts, socks,

and T-shirts and

throwing them

into the suitcase

on her bed. A

swimsuit even

landed on Peggy's

head!

"Where are they . . . ," muttered Chloe,
searching through all her drawers. "Mum!"
she hollered down the stairs. "I can't find
my goggles!"

"Check the cupboard in the hall!" Mum
called back.

After stepping over Peggy, Chloe ran out of the room to look for her goggles.

Peggy wandered into the hallway.

"Dad!" shouted Finn, bursting out of his room. "I can't find my fishing net!"

"It might be in the shed!" Dad called back to him.

Finn nearly trod on Peggy's paw as he hurried past.

"Help!" yelled Ruby, dragging a bulging backpack out of her room. She was holding a tatty stuffed elephant in one hand. "I can't fit Mr. Flump into my backpack!"

"Excuse me, Peggy," said Mum, brushing

past her as she came upstairs. She looked at Ruby's bag and shook her head. "You can't take all of these, sweetie." Mum began pulling cuddly toys from Ruby's bag. Peggy had to climb over a plush dinosaur and a stuffed lion to get by.

Dad dashed past, holding the hamper. "Clean clothes coming through," he said, nearly tripping over Peggy.

Everyone was rushing around, frantically packing. No matter where Peggy sat, she always seemed to be in the way.

I'd better lie low for a bit, she thought. Peggy went back into Chloe's room and squeezed under the bed. Nobody would

step on her there! She shut her eyes, and soon dozed off.

When Peggy woke up, the house was quiet. Too quiet.

She wriggled out from under the bed and looked around. *Where is everyone?* Peggy wandered out into the hallway, but there was no sign of anyone. And all the suitcases were gone, too.

Starting to feel worried, Peggy went downstairs. But her family wasn't any-where to be seen.

Maybe they're packing up the car, she thought.

Jumping up onto the windowsill, she looked out at the driveway.

The car was gone.

They've gone on holiday without me! she realized in dismay. "Oh no!" she wailed. "They left me behind!" How would she survive for a whole week on her own?

Just then, a car sped down the road, swerved into the driveway, and stopped with a loud squeal of brakes. Chloe jumped out of the car, unlocked the front door, and ran inside.

"Peggy!" she cried.

Peggy ran to her friend and jumped into her arms, wriggling with joy. She licked Chloe's face all over. She had never been so relieved to see anyone in her entire life!

"I'm so sorry!" said Chloe. "We came back as soon as we realized we'd forgotten to pack the most important thing of all. . . ." Chloe gave Peggy a kiss. "You!"

Chapter Three

"Are we almost there?" asked Chloe, tapping her mum's shoulder.

"Not much farther to go," Mum said without taking her eyes off the road.

"I need to do a wee," said Ruby, squirming next to Peggy in the back seat.

Me too, thought Peggy. They had been driving for ages. It had been hours since they'd stopped for a picnic lunch at a rest area.

"Hold it in a bit longer," said Dad. "We're nearly there."

"Can we change the music?" moaned Finn. "If I have to listen to *The Little Mermaid* soundtrack one more time, I'm going to scream."

Dad changed the music to a rock band, and Finn pretended he was drumming along.

"Cut it out!" whined Chloe, shoving her brother's elbow out of the way. "Get off my side."

Before an all-out war could break out in the back seat, Dad turned around and said, "Look! You can see the sea in the distance."

Peggy stuck her head out the window to get a better view. Her ears flapped as the wind rushed against her face. Along with the usual car scents of gasoline and rubber, she could also smell something salty and a bit fishy in the air.

Mmmm, thought Peggy, sniffing.

"Left here," said Dad, and Mum steered the car off the highway and onto a road leading to the coast.

After passing through a few villages, they turned again, down a bumpy road. At the very end of it, Peggy could see something blue sparkling in the distance. The sea!

The road stopped at a little bay with two small stone cottages. Beyond them, a wooden path wound through the dunes, leading to a sandy beach.

"We're here!" cried Chloe.

Mum parked the car, and everyone tumbled out.

Aaah, thought Peggy, stretching out her hind legs. *That's better!*

"Which one is ours?" asked Ruby. One of the cottages was painted white and had wild roses climbing up the front. The other was gray and had colorful buoys and fishing nets piled up outside it.

"It must be this one," said Chloe, pointing to the white cottage. It had a little painted sign over the door that read MERMAID COTTAGE.

"The owner said it would be unlocked," said Mum.

"Me first!" cried Ruby, opening the door and running inside.

Peggy hurried in after her, with Chloe following right behind.

"Oh, it's adorable!" said Chloe, looking around, enchanted.

The living room was painted white, with blue curtains in the windows. In the middle was a wood-burning stove surrounded by worn but comfy-looking armchairs, and shelves stocked with books, board games, playing cards, and jigsaw puzzles. On the dining table was a jug filled with roses, and their sweet scent filled the whole cottage.

"I could use a hand with the luggage," said Dad, staggering in with two heavy suitcases.

"I'll help," said Finn. He hurried outside to get more bags from the trunk, while Peggy and the girls raced around, investigating.

The cottage had three bedrooms—one with a double bed for Mum and Dad, a tiny room with a single bed for Finn, and one with bunk beds for Chloe and Ruby.

"Mermaids!" gasped Chloe in delight. The girls' bedroom was decorated with mermaids everywhere. There were mermaids on the curtains, mermaids on the duvet covers, and a painting of a mermaid on the wall.

"I get the top bunk!" said Chloe.

"But I've never slept up high before," said Ruby, pouting.

"You're too little," said Chloe. "You might fall out of bed in the night."

"No I won't," Ruby protested.

The girls glared at each other, their arms crossed, each unwilling to give in.

Peggy gazed up at the top bunk apprehensively. She usually slept in Chloe's bed, but there was no way her little legs could get her up there! *I guess I'll have to sleep on the ground*, she thought sadly. She looked down at the floor and whimpered.

Chloe suddenly realized what was wrong. "Okay," she said, sitting down on the bottom bunk and patting her thighs so Peggy would jump onto her lap. "I guess you can have the top bunk, Ruby. Peggy and I will sleep down here."

Thank goodness! thought Peggy, licking Chloe's face. She should have known that her best friend would never let her down.

"Yay!" cheered Ruby, and scrambled up

the ladder and to arrange her cuddly toys on the top bunk.

"Ahoy there!" came a voice from outside the cottage, followed by a knock on the door.

Peggy and the girls hurried out to see who it was. A grizzled man with wild white hair stood on the doorstep, wearing rain boots and a plaid shirt, its sleeves pushed up to reveal a mermaid tattoo on his arm.

"You must be Captain Pete," said Dad, shaking his hand.

"Sorry I wasn't here when you got in," said Pete. "I was out on my boat." He held up a glistening silver fish. "I brought you a welcome gift."

"Oh, wow!" said Finn, impressed. "Did you really catch that yourself?"

"Aye," said Pete, nodding.

As Dad put the fish in the refrigerator, Mum introduced everyone, including Peggy.

Captain Pete whistled, and a huge dog bounded up from the beach. He had shaggy black fur and a red bandana tied around his neck. "This here is my first mate, Neptune."

Peggy had never seen such a big dog before. Neptune towered over her. "Hi,"

she said, wagging her curly tail to be
friendly. "Are you named after the planet?"
she asked, remembering what Chloe had
said about her science project.

"No," said Neptune, looking down at
her. "I'm named after the god of the sea."

"Oh," said Peggy, feeling a bit silly.
"Maybe we could play on the beach

together tomorrow," she suggested.

Neptune shook his head. "I can't, I'm afraid. Not all of us are on holiday, you know," he said. "I'm a working dog—I go out fishing with Captain Pete."

Now Peggy felt even sillier.

"Did you have any questions about the cottage?" asked Pete. "The plumbing can be a bit temperamental. Sometimes you need to jiggle the toilet handle when you flush it."

"I've got a question," Chloe said. "Have you ever seen a mermaid?"

The fisherman's eyes twinkled merrily. "Oh, aye," he said. "Lots of them. Why else do you think I named this place Mermaid Cottage?"

Ruby's eyes lit up and she clapped her hands in delight.

"I knew it!" said Chloe. She poked her brother in the ribs. "Told you so."

"What about sharks?" Finn asked. "When you're out at sea, do you see a lot of those too?"

Peggy hoped not!

But Pete reached into the neck of his sweater and pulled out a necklace made from a leather thong with a big, white tooth hanging from it. "I caught this one myself."

Finn whistled under his breath. "That is so cool," he said.

Ruby clutched Mum's hand, looking as scared as Peggy felt.

"Don't worry," said the fisherman, winking at her. "The bay is perfectly safe for swimming. I'll let you folks get settled in," he said. Then he whistled to Neptune and ambled over to the other cottage.

After everyone had unpacked, Dad fired up the barbecue and grilled the fish Pete had brought them. When it was cooked, they ate dinner outside, watching the sun set. It sank down toward the horizon like a ball of flames, making the water glow with orange light.

"This is the life," said Mum, sitting back in her deck chair and sighing contentedly.

"I really like it here," said Chloe, smiling at her mother.

Me too, thought Peggy happily. She gobbled up her last bit of grilled fish and licked her chops. So far, being on holiday was amazing!

Chapter Four

"Wake up! We're on holiday!"

Peggy, who was curled up next to Chloe, opened her eyes and saw Ruby's grinning face hanging down from the top bunk. Chloe sat up so quickly that she nearly bumped her head on the bed above. From the pale light streaming through the curtains, Peggy could tell it was still very early in the morning. But there was no time to waste—there was a beach to explore!

The girls jumped out of bed and quickly got dressed in their bathing suits. They hurried into the kitchen, where Finn and Dad were eating cereal at the little table.

"We want to go to the beach," said Chloe.

"Breakfast first," said Dad.

The girls bolted down their cereal while Finn poured some dry dog food into a bowl for Peggy.

"Let's go!" shouted Ruby when they'd finished eating and done the washing up.

Dad pressed a finger to his lips. "Shh! Mum's sleeping in," he said. "But I'll take you down to the beach."

After gathering up buckets and spades, towels, and beach chairs, they left the cottage and headed down the dune-lined path to the beach. Peggy's short legs sank into the soft, golden sand as they walked toward the water. It was low tide, so the waves lapping at the sand were gentle.

Because it was early, the beach was still empty. They set out their towels and chairs, and then they all ran down to the water's edge.

"There's Captain Pete!" said Finn, waving

to a fishing boat out in the bay. Neptune stood at the prow, looking very important.

Peggy barked hello to him, but either he didn't hear it over the noise of the boat—or he was just ignoring her.

"Let's look for shells," said Chloe, running along the beach.

"This one's pretty," said Ruby, picking up a fanned shell and adding it to her bucket.

"That's a cockleshell," said Dad.

The children found all sorts of empty shells—oysters, limpets, long razor clams, and spiral-shaped whelks. Soon their buckets were nearly full.

"We're never going to be able to take all

of these home," Dad said, chuckling.

Peggy saw something black on the sand and gave it an inquisitive sniff. At first she thought it was a big bug, but it wasn't moving. She barked, and everyone came running over.

"Peggy found a mermaid's purse," said Dad.

"Really?" said Chloe, picking it up and studying it excitedly. "There must be mermaids around here if one of them left her handbag behind."

Dad laughed and shook his head. "A mermaid's purse is actually a pouch for shark eggs. This one's all dried out, though."

"Ugh," said Chloe, looking disappointed.

Sharks? thought Peggy, glancing out at the waves nervously.

"Cool!" said Finn, taking the mermaid's purse off Chloe.

Wandering farther along the beach, they came to some shallow pools surrounded by rocks covered in barnacles and seaweed.

"Let's see if we can find any crabs," said Finn.

The children waded into the water and crouched down, peering among the rocks and slippery strands of seaweed.

Peggy noticed something moving behind a rock. Curious, she dipped her paw into the water and nudged the rock. Then—*SNAP!* Something pinched her paw!

"Ouch!" yelped Peggy.

"Do you mind?" snapped a crab, staring

at her with bulging eyes. "This is my home."

"Sorry," said Peggy, scurrying away. So far, sea creatures didn't seem very friendly!

The children brought their buckets of shells back to their towels. By now, the sun had risen high in the clear, blue sky. The tide was beginning to come in, and the beach had filled with other families.

"I'm hot," said Chloe. "Let's go swimming. That will cool us off."

"Last one in's a rotten egg!" cried Finn, pulling off his T-shirt. He sprinted down to the water and dived straight in.

Chloe and Ruby held hands and ran, squealing, into the foamy, white waves. As Chloe floated on her back, riding the waves, Ruby paddled through the water proudly.

"Look, Daddy!" she called over to Dad, who had waded in up to his knees. "I'm swimming all on my own."

"Don't go out too deep, Rubes," he warned her.

"Come on in, Peggy," shouted Chloe. "The water's lovely!"

Peggy longed to play with the children, but she was too scared to go in. The waves were very big now. And there might be crabs—or worse, *sharks*—in the sea. Standing at the edge of the water, Peggy watched Chloe, Finn, and Ruby splashing about. She kept her eyes peeled for a mermaid. She knew how badly Chloe wanted to see one.

A seagull waddled over to Peggy. "Hey there, Four Legs," she squawked. "Watcha lookin' for?"

"A mermaid," said Peggy. "Do you know where I could find one?"

"Can't say I've seen any recently," said the seagull. "But I can tell you a good joke: Why did the mermaid blush?"

"Um, I'm not sure," said Peggy.

"Because the sea *weed*," replied the seagull, flapping her wings in amusement. "Get it? I'm Pearl, by the way," she said.

"I'm Peggy," said Peggy, glad to have someone to talk to.

As Pearl pecked at the sand, searching for food, she told Peggy more jokes. "Why did the fish cross the ocean?" Pearl didn't even bother waiting for a reply. "To get to the other *tide*." She let out a loud squawk of laughter.

At lunchtime, Mum wandered down to the beach with a picnic hamper. The children came running out of the water, dripping wet.

After wrapping themselves up in fluffy towels, they flopped down onto the picnic blanket. Peggy came over to join them.

"I'm starving," said Chloe.

"Me too," said Finn.

"It must be the sea air," said Mum, handing out sandwiches, potato chips and apples.

"Mmm," said Pearl, eyeing the picnic hungrily. "That sure looks good."

Chloe threw a few chips to Peggy's new friend. Pearl gobbled them up before any other seagulls could swoop down and get them.

"Don't encourage them," scolded Mum, shooing the gull away with her hands. She took out a bottle of lotion from her bag. "Everyone needs to put on more sunscreen."

"Yuck, it feels cold," said Ruby, squirming as Mum rubbed the lotion onto her back. A drop fell onto Peggy's nose. It smelled like coconut.

"You've got to put it on, Rubes," said Mum. "Otherwise your skin will burn."

Mum put some on Chloe next, but when she tried to put some on Finn, he pulled away. "I'm not a baby—I can do it myself."

"Can I go swimming again?" asked Chloe as soon as she'd finished eating.

"Not yet," said Mum. "You need to digest your food."

"What are we going to do if we can't go swimming?" said Chloe.

"When I walked down to the beach, I noticed a sign for a sand sculpture competition," said Mum.

"Ooh! Let's enter it!" said Ruby.

"What should we make?" asked Dad.

"A shark," said Finn.

"They're making a shark already," said Mum, pointing to a family farther down the beach who had started making a great white out of sand.

"I've got an idea," said Chloe. "Let's make a mermaid!"

The whole family got to work. Peggy

wanted to help, too, so she dug through the sand with her paws. Sand flew everywhere!

"Er, thanks, Peggy," laughed Chloe, shaking sand out of her hair.

They started shaping the mermaid's body. Dad and the girls worked on the mermaid's long tail, patting the damp sand into place with their hands, while Mum and Finn made her head, arms, and tummy.

"We can use seaweed for her hair," said Chloe. Peggy ran along the beach, picking up long, slimy strands of seaweed in her mouth, and then brought them back for Chloe to drape on the mermaid's head.

"Let's decorate her with pretty pebbles

and the shells we found this morning," said Ruby, lugging her bucket of shells over.

As her family added shells to the mermaid's tail, Peggy wandered down the beach, checking out the competition. The team who had made the shark had used white pebbles for teeth. Even though she knew it wasn't real, Peggy couldn't help shivering. One family had made a huge sandcastle that looked like something from a fairy tale. It had four pointy turrets and a drawbridge made of Popsicle sticks. Another group had built a gigantic octopus, and others had made a pirate ship, using an empty potato chip bag for a flag.

All the sculptures were really good, but Peggy thought her family's mermaid was by far the best.

When she got back, the sand mermaid was holding like a handbag the mermaid's purse they'd found that morning. Her tail was covered in shells, making it look like she really had scales.

"Quick, we need to finish soon," said Mum, checking her watch. "The competition ends at four o'clock."

The judge walked up and down the beach holding a clipboard. He inspected all the sand sculptures, jotting down notes. Then everyone gathered around as he announced the results.

"This was a really difficult decision," said the judge. "All of the sand sculptures are wonderful. But first prize goes to . . . the mermaid!"

Everyone clapped as Chloe and her

family collected their prize—a blue rosette and a gift voucher to the local mini-golf course. Peggy barked happily over the applause. She was so proud of her family!

"We did it, Peggy!" Chloe said, attaching the rosette to her collar.

Then Dad asked the judge to take a photo of the whole family posing with the sand mermaid.

"What a perfect day," said Mum as they started to gather up their beach things.

Chloe nodded as she folded up a beach chair. "The only thing that could have made it even better is seeing a *real* mermaid!"

I'll find one for you, thought Peggy. They still had six more days of holiday—and she would keep looking until she found a mermaid for Chloe. She would do anything to make her best friend happy!

Chapter Five

"Muuuuuum!" wailed Finn the next morning.

Peggy, Chloe, and Ruby ran out of their bedroom to see what was wrong.

Finn stood in the kitchen wearing just his pajama bottoms. His face, chest, arms, and back were bright pink.

"Oh dear," said Mum. "You must not have put on enough sunscreen yesterday. You've gotten sunburned."

"You look like a tomato," Chloe said, giggling.

"Your nose is red like a clown's," said Ruby, pointing as Finn glowered at them.

"Girls, that's not very nice," said Dad.

Mum found some soothing aloe lotion to put on Finn's sunburnt skin. He winced as she spread it on. Peggy felt glad she didn't need to worry about sunburn, thanks to her fur. Finn's sunburn looked very painful!

"We'd better stay off the beach today,"

Mum said. "We can explore the harbor instead."

After breakfast, Dad drove everyone into the village center. The cobbled streets were lined with quaint tea rooms, souvenir shops, and fish-and-chip shops. The delicious smells wafting out of them made Peggy's tummy rumble.

They wandered over to the crescent-shaped harbor to look at the boats.

"Hey, there's Captain Pete," said Finn.

The fisherman waved to them from the pier, where he was unloading his catch. Neptune helped him drag nets full of glistening fish onto the dock.

"Need any help?" Peggy barked.

The big black dog looked up at her and shook his head. "No thanks. I've got this."

Peggy sighed. Neptune was helping his owner with a very important job. She wanted to be helpful, too. Then she remembered what Chloe had said the day before. Peggy *did* have a job—finding a mermaid for Chloe.

A man in a pirate costume stood by the harbor wall, ringing a bell. "Hear ye! Hear ye!" he called. "There's a free storytelling session starting in five minutes."

"Ooh! That sounds great," said Mum, herding everyone over to where a small audience was beginning to form.

The pirate stood on a wooden crate, cleared his throat, and adjusted his tricorn hat. Then he began his story. "Today I'm going to tell you a local legend. It's about a sailor and"—he paused dramatically—"a mermaid!"

Finn groaned, but Chloe and Ruby exchanged excited looks.

Peggy cocked her ears and listened to the story, about a sailor who heard beautiful singing coming from the beach at night. He discovered that the singer was a mermaid sitting on a rock, just off the shore.

The audience listened, captivated, as the

storyteller described the mermaid. "She had glittering silver scales that reflected the moonlight, long green hair with rippling waves, and a voice as sweet as a choir of angels. . . ."

"She sounds beautiful," Chloe whispered to Ruby.

The storyteller told them how the sailor fell in love with the mermaid and followed her out to sea. He was never seen in the village again. When the storyteller finished speaking, everyone applauded.

"I wonder what happened to the sailor?" said Chloe as they walked over to the mini-golf course along the seafront.

"He was probably eaten by a shark," said Finn, smirking.

"No he wasn't!" said Ruby. "The mermaid took him to her underwater palace and made him king of all the sea creatures."

At the mini-golf course, Dad handed over their voucher, and everyone—apart from Peggy—got a golf club and a ball.

"This one matches your nose," Chloe said, handing Finn a red ball.

"Ha ha," he said. "Red's my lucky color. I'm going to win."

The first hole had a lighthouse at the end of it. Chloe went first, tapping a blue ball with her club. The ball rolled down the green carpet and stopped just short of the hole.

"Aww!" said Chloe, disappointed. "It nearly went in."

Wanting to help, Peggy bounded forward

and picked up the ball in her mouth.

"No, Peggy!" everyone cried.

Too late. Peggy dropped the ball right into the hole.

"Hole in one!" laughed Dad.

"That's cheating!" protested Finn.

"Naughty Peggy," scolded Chloe. "You mustn't move the balls."

Oops! Peggy felt bad. She'd just been trying to help.

As her family played golf, Peggy was careful not to touch the balls again— even though she was tempted to chase after them. Each hole had a different seaside theme—there were pirate ships and treasure chests and whales. Finally they came to a hole with a big shark figure.

Peggy eyed it nervously, but it didn't move—even when Ruby accidentally whacked it with her golf club.

Finn tapped his red ball, and it rolled

through the shark's open jaws and plopped into the cup at the end. "Yes!" He danced around, celebrating his hole in one. "That puts me in the lead," he cheered.

When they got to the end of the course, a familiar seagull was perched on top of the giant squid at the last hole. "Hey, Four Legs, how many tickles does it take to make an octopus laugh?" she squawked.

"Hi, Pearl," Peggy said to her friend from the beach. She counted the octopus's legs and guessed the answer. "Is it eight?"

"No. Ten tickles. *Tentacles*, get it?" The seagull hopped up and down, laughing,

Then she asked, "Hey, are you still looking for a mermaid?"

"Yes," said Peggy.

"I've just seen one," said Pearl. "On the high street."

Peggy barked and tugged on her lead eagerly. "Come on!" she told Chloe. "We need to go—NOW!"

"I guess Peggy's had enough mini golf," Dad said, chuckling.

Peggy pranced impatiently as her family finished up their game and returned their golf clubs. When they were back on the promenade, Peggy looked around. Where was the mermaid?

"She's over there!" squawked Pearl, gesturing with her wing as she circled overhead.

In the distance, Peggy saw something shiny glittering in the sun—the mermaid's tail!

Peggy tugged so hard on her lead that Chloe lost her grip. Her lead dragging behind her, Peggy raced down the street, as fast as her little legs could go.

Every so often, the mermaid stopped and handed a piece of paper to someone walking past. Panting hard, Peggy finally caught up with her, just outside a souvenir shop.

"Gotcha!" Peggy said, biting the mermaid's tail to stop her from getting away.

"Whoa!" cried the mermaid. Her arms windmilled around wildly as she lost her balance and knocked over a display of beach balls. The balls bounced all over the street, and the mermaid landed on her bottom. The pieces of paper she'd been holding flew through the air and fluttered down onto the cobblestones. One of them landed next to Peggy. It had a picture of an ice cream cone on it.

"Peggy!" shouted Chloe, running over and picking her up. "What's gotten into you today?"

"I'm so sorry," said Dad, helping the mermaid up to her feet.

Huh? thought Peggy, confused. *Mermaids don't have feet. . . .*

As the mermaid stood up and brushed herself off, Peggy realized that she hadn't found a mermaid. She'd found someone dressed up as a mermaid.

"I guess your dog really wants an ice cream," said the mermaid, smiling. She handed Dad one of her pieces of paper.

"'The Frosty Mermaid,'" he said, reading the leaflet out loud.

"This coupon gets you a discount on ice creams," said the mermaid. She pointed to a shop a bit farther down the road. "The store is just there."

"Ooh! Can we get one?" asked Ruby.

"Not now," said Mum. "You'll spoil your lunch."

Chloe, Finn, and Ruby helped the lady in the mermaid costume gather up all her leaflets, while Mum and Dad collected the brightly colored beach balls, and put them back into a wire bin outside the souvenir shop. Peggy tried to help too, but the balls kept rolling away.

"Sorry again," said Dad.

"No harm done," said the mermaid lady, patting Peggy on the head. "Do pop in for an ice cream sometime."

"Can we go into the souvenir shop?" Chloe asked, peering into the window.

"I suppose it's the least we can do," Mum said. "But you'd better keep hold of Peggy so she can't knock anything else over."

Peggy felt so ashamed. She had thought she'd found a mermaid for Chloe, but instead she'd just made a mess.

The children had taken their pocket

money on holiday, and they spent ages browsing in the souvenir shop. It wasn't very big, but it was crammed with postcards, sticks of rock candy, windmills, colorful beach toys, and trinkets made from seashells.

Mum chose a pair of sunglasses with mirrored lenses.

"Very cool," said Dad, winking at her as he tried on a straw sun hat.

Finn picked out a fishing net for himself and an eraser shaped like a shark for his friend Zach.

"I just can't decide which one," said Ruby, struggling to choose between an inflatable swimming toy that looked like a doughnut with pink sprinkles and a float shaped like a Popsicle.

But Chloe didn't have any trouble deciding. She knew exactly what she wanted—a silver necklace with a charm shaped like a mermaid.

When Ruby finally decided on the inflatable doughnut, they paid for their purchases and left the shop.

Outside, Mum helped Chloe put her new necklace on straightaway.

"It's so pretty," Chloe said, looking down at the little mermaid sparkling around her neck.

But Peggy knew it was a *real* mermaid that Chloe wanted. If Peggy couldn't find one, there was no other option—she would just have to become a mermaid herself!

Chapter Six

That night, after dinner, Dad got out a deck of cards and started to shuffle them. "What game should we play?" he asked the others.

"How about rummy?" said Finn.

"That's too hard!" said Ruby. "Let's play Snap."

"I've got a better idea," said Chloe. "We're at the seaside—Let's play Go Fish!"

As her family played card games, Peggy tried to work out how she was going to become a mermaid. In the film *The Little Mermaid*, a sea witch had used magic to make the mermaid a human. Maybe a sea witch could also turn a pug into a mermaid? Peggy shuddered. Sea witches were scary. There had to be a better way!

She suddenly remembered the story she'd heard at the harbor. The storyteller had said that mermaids sang at night. A plan began to form in Peggy's head. *I'll wait until everyone is asleep*, she decided, *and then I'll become a mermaid!*

Peggy glanced over at her family, wondering if they were nearly ready for bed. Ruby yawned and rested her head on the table. Peggy felt sleepy too. It had been a busy day. But she knew she needed to stay awake.

"I win!" announced Chloe, slapping her cards down on the table.

"Well done," said Mum, giving her a high five. "Let's tidy up now. It's bedtime."

"Awww," said Chloe. "But we're on holiday."

"Yeah," said Finn. "I want a rematch."

"We can play again tomorrow," said Dad, picking up Ruby and carrying her into the girls' bedroom, as Mum gathered up the cards.

After Chloe had brushed her teeth and changed into her pajamas, she climbed into the bottom bunk. "Sweet dreams, Peggy," she said, giving the pug a kiss good night. Then she rolled over and closed her eyes.

Peggy listened to Chloe's breathing become slow and steady, and soon she could tell that her friend was fast asleep. Straining her ears, Peggy heard Dad gargling in the bathroom and Mum turning the pages of her book in the next room. Eventually she heard the sound she was waiting for—*CLICK!*—as Mum and Dad turned off their bedroom light.

Peggy waited a while longer, until she was sure everyone was asleep. Then she hopped down from Chloe's bed and padded out into the hall.

Mermaid Cottage was dark and silent, apart from Dad's snoring coming from the grown-ups' bedroom. When she got to the front door, Peggy hesitated. It was very dark outside. What if she got lost and fell into the sea and was eaten by a shark? For a moment, Peggy wanted to crawl back into bed and snuggle up with Chloe.

You're doing this for her, she reminded herself. Peggy owed so much to Chloe, who loved and cared for her. Now it was Peggy's turn to help her friend. Chloe really wanted to see a mermaid, so Peggy needed to make that happen.

She tried to nudge the door open with her paw, but it was locked. Luckily, the living room window was open a bit to let in the cool night air. Peggy climbed up on a chair and squeezed through the gap. Then she jumped down, and her paws landed on soft sand. She was outside!

Oh wow! she thought, staring up in amazement.

Back at home, there weren't nearly so many stars in the night sky. Here, away from the city lights, the inky black sky sparkled with tiny pinpricks of light. Peggy thought about Chloe's solar system project. It was hard to believe that way up in the universe, there were enormous planets, too. As she looked up, a comet blazed across the sky, leaving a glittering trail of white behind it. Then Peggy saw a shooting star—and another! Peggy's fur stood on end as she watched the stars dance like fireworks across the sky. Tonight there was magic in the air. Anything felt possible—even a pug becoming a mermaid!

Once her eyes had adjusted to the dark, Peggy got to work. She hurried down to the beach and found some slimy strands of seaweed and draped them over her head. There! Now she had long, green hair.

But mermaids also had tails. . . .

Peggy glanced around, looking for something to use as a tail. Outside Captain Pete's cottage, there was a jumble of fishing nets.

Aha! thought Peggy. Those would be perfect!

She dragged one of the nets over with her teeth and arranged it around her hind legs like a tail. Now that she looked like a mermaid, it was time to sing. After taking a deep breath, Peggy began to howl. *AROOOOOOOO! ARRRR-ROOOOOOOOOO! ARRRRRRRR-ROOOOOOOOOO!*

Lights switched on in Mermaid Cottage, and then in the fisherman's cottage next door. Peggy sang her heart out, hoping she sounded as beautiful as the mermaid in the story.

One by one, Peggy's family stumbled

outside in their pajamas. Captain Pete came out in his dressing gown, too, with Neptune by his side.

"Peggy?" said Chloe, squinting at her through the dark.

Peggy's heart sank. Chloe didn't think she was a mermaid. She'd recognized her straightaway.

"Oh, you poor thing," said Chloe, scooping her up. She picked the seaweed off Peggy's head and threw it onto the ground. "Ugh!" she said. "That stinks."

"I'm so sorry she woke you up," Mum apologized to Captain Pete. "I have no idea how she got out."

"She must have gotten tangled up in one of your fishing nets," said Dad, returning the net to Pete.

"No worries," said Pete, chuckling. "I'm glad she's okay. When I heard all that howling, I thought she'd injured herself."

They all went back inside their cottages. Peggy tried to climb onto Chloe's bed, but Mum shooed her out of the bedroom. "You're sleeping on the floor tonight,

Peggy," she said, shutting the door. "You smell terrible."

Curled up on the hard floor, Peggy felt ashamed. She'd woken everybody up in the middle of the night—and all for nothing. If she couldn't become a mermaid on a magical night like tonight, when *could* she?

After breakfast the next morning, they trooped down to the beach. While Dad set out the blankets and beach umbrella, Mum spread sunscren on everyone. This time Finn didn't protest. As Mum and Dad settled down in the umbrella's shade to read their books, Peggy looked around for someone to play with.

She tried Finn first, nudging him with her paw. "Sorry, Peggy," he said, putting on his headphones. "I'm just not in the mood to play."

Next, Peggy went over to Ruby, who was lying on a beach towel, her eyes shut. Peggy licked her cheek, and Ruby opened one eye. "I'm taking a nap," she murmured sleepily.

Peggy went over to Chloe and tugged on her swimsuit playfully. Chloe looked up from the text message she was writing and shook her head. "Maybe later, Peggy," she said. "I'm sending a message to Ellie. She says Coco is doing well."

Dejected, Peggy wandered down to the water and stared out at the sea. Nobody wanted to play with her, and she only had herself to blame. It was all her fault everyone was so tired. She had to make it up to them somehow. Maybe she could still find a mermaid. And there was one likely place where she hadn't looked yet—in the water.

Gathering her courage, Peggy waded into the sea, her paws sinking into the sand as water swirled around her short legs. She went in a bit deeper, until the water reached up to her tummy. *Brrr!* It was a bit chilly. A big wave swelled in the distance. It curled and came rushing toward the beach. Crashing over Peggy's head, it knocked her off her paws and dragged her underwater.

Salty water stung Peggy's eyes and went up her nose. She kicked her paws frantically, trying to fight her way back to the beach. But the waves were much too strong. They kept sucking her down, under the water's surface!

"Help!" Peggy yelped, swallowing a mouthful of water. She felt herself being pulled farther and farther away from the beach by the tide.

Then, out of nowhere, something picked

her up by the scruff of her neck, the way her mum had carried her when she was a puppy. A moment later, it set her down gently on the warm sand. Peggy looked up and saw her savior—Neptune.

The big dog towered over her, looking cross. "What were you trying to do?" he growled. "Drown?"

"No!" she spluttered. "I was trying to find a mermaid."

"A mermaid, eh?" Understanding flickered in Neptune's wise brown eyes. "Is that what last night was all about too?" he asked her.

Peggy nodded sheepishly. "Chloe loves mermaids," she explained. "Last night I tried to become a mermaid, but when that didn't work, I decided I needed to find one for her in the water. You probably think I'm stupid, right?"

Neptune shook his head sympathetically. "You were just trying to help your friend. I'd do anything for Captain Pete, too. But you shouldn't go into the water if you don't know how to swim."

Peggy sighed. "I guess I'll never find a mermaid for Chloe now."

"Look," said Neptune, "I don't know anything about finding mermaids. But I *can* teach you how to swim."

"Really?" asked Peggy.

"Of course," said Neptune. "Ever heard of the doggy paddle? They named it after us for a reason."

Peggy looked out at the sea anxiously. The waves were VERY big. What if they pulled her under again? She might get swept out to sea, where a shark could eat her. She would never see Chloe again. . . .

"I'll keep you safe," promised Neptune. "I'm a Newfoundland dog. We've got waterproof fur and special webbed paws to help us swim." He held up his front paw to show her. "That's why fishermen take us out on their boats—because we're life-savers."

"That's really cool," said Peggy.

"Come on," said Neptune. "Let's get started."

First Peggy needed to get used to getting her face wet. "Good girl," Neptune said as she lowered her face into the foamy waves.

"That tickles," Peggy said, giggling.

When she was ready, they went out a bit deeper. "Don't worry, I've got you," Neptune said. Peggy used her teeth to hold on to his shaggy fur as he towed her through the water. "Kick your back paws," he coached her. Peggy did what he said. "Now your front paws . . . and . . . let go," said Neptune.

Peggy felt scared, but she let go of Neptune's fur and paddled her legs furiously. Instead of sinking, she was swimming!

Peggy paddled up and down the beach, holding her head above the waves. "I can do it!" she yipped happily. "I can doggy paddle!"

"Well done!" barked Neptune.

"Way to go, Peggy!" called Pearl, flying overhead.

The barking and squawking attracted everyone's attention.

"Look!" cried Chloe, running down to

the water, with Finn and Ruby following close behind her. "Peggy's swimming!"

The children ran into the water, and soon they were all splashing and playing in the waves. Peggy couldn't believe she'd been too scared to go into the sea before. Swimming was so much fun!

Ruby blew bubbles into the water, and Peggy chased after them, popping them with her paws.

"I'm so proud of you," said Chloe, stroking Peggy's damp head.

"I'll leave you to it," said Neptune, getting out of the water and shaking himself off. Water glistened on his thick, black fur.

"Thank you so much," said Peggy, her big eyes shining with gratitude. "You saved my life."

"I was just doing my job," said Neptune, winking. "Good luck finding a mermaid."

But Peggy had found something even more exciting than a mermaid—a hero!

Chapter Seven

Over the next few days, Peggy had lots of fun playing in the sea with Chloe, Ruby, and Finn. She loved being in the water now! They jumped over waves, had swimming races, and floated on Ruby's inflatable ring. No matter what they were doing, Peggy always kept a lookout for the silvery flash of a mermaid's tail. She saw plenty of little fish, and once she even spotted a seal sticking his whiskered face out of the water, but she still hadn't seen a mermaid.

On the last day of their holiday, Peggy stood on the sand, gentle waves lapping at her paws, and stared out at the sea. *I've got to find a mermaid for Chloe,* she thought. Time was running out—they were going home the next day!

A seagull swooped down and landed next to Peggy. "What's wrong, Four Legs?" Pearl squawked.

"I'm looking for a mermaid," said Peggy, peering into the distance.

"Still? I thought I found one for you in town," said Pearl.

Peggy shook her head sadly. "That wasn't a real mermaid," she told the seagull. "Just someone dressed up in a costume."

"That's a shame," said Pearl. "But I've got a new joke that might cheer you up. What did the sea say to the sand?"

Peggy looked down at the damp sand. "Er—"

"Nothing!" squawked Pearl. "It just WAVED!"

But Pearl's joke didn't make Peggy feel

better. She turned and looked at Chloe, who was building a sandcastle with Ruby farther up the beach. The thing her friend wanted most from this holiday was to see a mermaid. Peggy had promised to help her find one, but she had failed.

"The beach is pretty crowded at this time of year," said Pearl, eyeing a toddler holding a tuna sandwich. "Mermaids are shy. They're probably keeping well away."

Of course! thought Peggy. The beach was full of families swimming, sunbathing, and enjoying picnics. No wonder she hadn't seen a mermaid!

The little boy dropped his sandwich on

the ground. "Gotta go!" said Pearl. The seagull swooped over, snatched the sandwich with her beak, and flew away with her prize.

Peggy gazed out at the sea, which seemed to stretch endlessly into the distance. Mermaids were somewhere way out there. But how could she get to them? She was a good swimmer now, but her short legs could only doggy paddle so far. . . .

Just then, Chloe ran up to Peggy. "Guess what?" she cried. "Captain Pete has invited us to go fishing on his boat!"

Peggy let out an excited bark. This was perfect—a boat would take her far out to sea, where she could find a mermaid! Wagging her tail, she hurried back to the others with Chloe.

Pete's boat was anchored at the far end of the beach, bobbing in the shallows. Neptune was already on board, keeping lookout by the prow. He barked in greeting when he saw them approaching the boat.

"Welcome aboard!" said Pete, reaching down to help them climb into the boat. Chloe passed Peggy up to the captain, then hauled herself onto the deck.

"I'm going to catch the biggest fish," boasted Finn.

"No, I am!" said Chloe.

Peggy didn't care about catching fish. She just wanted to catch sight of a mermaid!

Captain Pete handed out life jackets to everyone.

"I don't need one of these," said Ruby. "I know how to swim."

"Everyone needs to wear one," said Pete firmly. "I don't want Neptune to have to jump in and rescue you."

Peggy knew they'd all be safe with Neptune to look after them, but she was glad to see Ruby put on her life jacket. Pete raised the anchor and switched on the engine,

and the boat chugged out to sea. Peggy
rested her paws on the side of the boat,
enjoying the feel of sea spray on her furry
face. She watched as the people on the
beach grew smaller and smaller. Eventually
they disappeared from view completely.

As the group went into deeper water, the wind picked up. The fishing boat rocked on the waves, and Peggy's tummy began to churn. She wasn't the only one feeling seasick—Dad and Ruby both looked a bit green as they gripped the railing.

"Ugggghhhhh!" Peggy moaned, staggering around the deck queasily.

"Don't worry," said Neptune. "You'll soon find your sea legs."

Peggy collapsed on

a pile of fishing nets and closed her eyes. But Neptune was right. It didn't take long to get used to the rocking motion. By the time Captain Pete switched off the engine, Peggy's stomach had settled.

"What do you think, Neptune?" asked Pete. "Does this look like a good spot?"

Neptune barked his approval.

Captain Pete dropped the anchor, then handed out fishing rods to his guests and taught them how to cast their lines.

"Oops!" Chloe giggled as she accidentally hooked Dad's shorts. "Told you I was going to catch a big one."

"You won't catch anything without

some bait," said Pete. He opened up his tackle box to reveal worms wriggling and squirming inside.

"Ew!" said Finn. Now HE looked a bit green. "That's so gross."

"Don't be such a wimp," said Chloe, putting a worm on the end of her line.

As her family threw their fishing lines into the water and waited to see if anything bit, Peggy scanned the waves, looking for a mermaid. To her disappointment, the only things she could see were a few sailing boats in the distance and some seagulls bobbing on the waves.

"I think I've got a nibble!" shouted Chloe.

Captain Pete pressed a finger to his lips. "You need to be quiet or you'll scare all the fish away."

"Sorry!" whispered Chloe.

"Okay, let's see what you've got," said Pete, helping Chloe reel in her fishing line. A small silver fish dangled from the end of it.

"We need to throw it back," said Pete, unhooking the fish. He tossed it into the water.

"Why?" asked Chloe.

"It's just a tiddler," said Pete. "We only keep the big ones. It's important to let the little fish grow up. That way there will always be plenty of fish in the sea."

A while later, Ruby's line jerked. Something was tugging at the end of it!

"Help!" Ruby called, struggling to keep hold of her fishing rod. Neptune hurried over and bit the bottom of her life jacket so she didn't go overboard.

"It must be a big one!" said Finn. He handed his fishing rod to Dad and helped Ruby reel in her line.

"Easy does it," coached Pete.

Suddenly there was a flash of silver as Finn and Ruby pulled a sea bass out of the water.

"Oh wow!" said Finn.

"Now, this one is a keeper," said Pete.

"I thought it was going to pull me into the water!" said Ruby.

"I've got to get a picture of that," said Mum, taking out her phone. As Ruby and Finn posed proudly with their fish, its scales gleaming in the sunlight, something in the water caught Peggy's eye. She ran over to the side of the boat and peered over the railing. Could it really be . . . ?

A shimmering silver fin stuck out of

the water. It was a mermaid's tail!

Peggy jumped up onto Chloe's legs, trying to get her attention. "Look in the water!" she barked, hoping Chloe would notice the mermaid.

"Shh!" Chloe scolded her. "You'll scare the fish away."

"What's wrong?" Neptune asked Peggy.

"Nothing!" said Peggy. "I've just seen a mermaid!"

She ran back to the side of the boat, but the silver mermaid tail had disappeared under the water. *Oh no! Where has it gone?* Peggy looked around wildly, and then she spotted the silver fin slicing through the water. The mermaid was getting away!

"Come back!" she barked.

There was no time to lose—she had to stop the mermaid. Without even pausing to think, Peggy climbed over the side of the boat . . . and dived into the sea!

Chapter Eight

SPLASH! Peggy hit the water and sank down . . . down . . . down. The water was a lot colder and deeper this far out at sea! Kicking her legs, she swam up to the surface and gasped for breath.

"Hey wait!" she called, spotting the

mermaid's silver tail fin in the distance. She swam toward it through the choppy waves.

To Peggy's relief, the fin turned and started moving toward her. As it got closer, a long, gray shape emerged from the water. Peggy gasped in terror. It wasn't a mermaid. It was a shark—and it was coming for her!

"Help!" howled Peggy. "A shark is going to eat me!"

A face with beady eyes and a pointed nose popped out of the water and regarded Peggy with amusement. "Who are you calling a shark?" she said, laughing. "I'm a dolphin."

"Are you going to eat me?" Peggy asked nervously. The dolphin seemed friendly, but when she opened her mouth, Peggy saw sharp white teeth.

"That depends," teased the dolphin in a squeaky voice. "What kind of fish are you?"

"I'm not a fish," said Peggy. "I'm a pug. My name's Peggy."

"I'm Misty," said the dolphin. "Don't

worry, I'm not going to eat you. You're much too furry!"

Peggy's relief at not being eaten soon turned to disappointment, as she realized she had jumped overboard for no reason. Blinking back tears, she turned and looked at the boat.

Chloe was leaning over the side, looking frantic with worry. "Dog overboard!" she cried, pointing at Peggy.

Captain Pete got a life ring and threw it into the water.

Neptune peered over the railing. "Need me to come and rescue you?" he barked down to Peggy.

"No, I'm fine," she called back. But her legs were beginning to feel very tired from treading water. "I don't suppose you could give me a lift back to the boat?" she asked Misty.

"Of course," said the dolphin. "Hop onto my back!"

Peggy scrambled onto the dolphin's slippery back and balanced like a surfer. "Whee!" she shouted in delight as the dolphin raced through the water.

"So, did you fall overboard?" asked Misty.

"No, I jumped in," explained Peggy. "I was trying to find a mermaid for my friend Chloe. Do you know where I could find one?"

Misty shook her head. "Can't say I've ever seen one."

Peggy sighed. "It's our last day of holiday, and I really wanted to make it special for Chloe."

Misty cocked her head to the side thoughtfully. "*Hmm*. My pod might be able to help with that. . . ."

When they reached the life ring, Peggy clutched it with her paws and Captain Pete pulled her back up to the boat.

"This is definitely the catch of the day," said Captain Pete, chuckling. Peggy shook herself dry, splattering everyone with drops of water.

"Oh, Peggy," said Chloe, picking her up and hugging her. "I was so scared that I was going to lose you."

"That dolphin saved her," said Ruby, pointing at Misty.

Out in the water, the dolphin made some high-pitched whistling and clicking noises. A few minutes later, a whole pod of dolphins surrounded Misty, water glistening on their smooth, silver backs as their long mouths chattered excitedly.

"Look at all of them!" gasped Chloe.

"Listen up, everybody," Misty said to the other dolphins. She gestured toward the boat with her fin. "Let's give Peggy the pug and her friend Chloe a special show they'll never forget!"

The dolphins clicked and slapped their fins against the water. Then they all shot forward and jumped up high, their sleek bodies arcing above the sea. They raced through the waves, leaping again and again as they swam around the boat. Peggy and her family watched in awe as the dolphins did flips and twists in the air, as graceful as ballet dancers. For their grand finale, the dolphins slapped the water with their tail fins, cheekily splashing the humans on the boat.

"The dolphins got me wet," said Ruby,

giggling and wiping drops of water off her face.

"That was the coolest thing I've ever seen," said Finn with a huge grin.

"It was awesome," Chloe said breathlessly.

"How was that?" Misty called up to Peggy. "Special enough for you?"

"That was amazing," said Peggy. "Thank you so much!"

"No problem," said Misty, waving good-bye with her fin.

The dolphins swam off. Peggy and her family watched them leaping through the water until they'd vanished into the distance.

"Wow," said Chloe, cuddling Peggy tight. "Just . . . wow."

That evening, Dad grilled on the barbecue the fish Ruby had caught, and they invited Captain Pete and Neptune to join them for dinner. Even though she wasn't invited, Pearl came too, swooping down to gobble up any bits of food that fell on the ground.

As they sat outside, eating fish and corn on the cob, all anyone could talk about was the dolphins.

"In all my years at sea, I've never seen anything like that before," said Captain Pete, shaking his head.

"It was spectacular," said Mum.

"Unforgettable," agreed Dad.

Neptune and Peggy lay next to each other, basking in the warm rays of the setting sun.

Pearl waddled over to the two dogs. "Hey, where do dolphins sleep?" she asked them.

"I know!" said Peggy, guessing the punch line. "On a sea bed!"

Cackling, the seagull hurried off to snatch a piece of fish Ruby had dropped on the ground.

"That was pretty impressive swimming today," said Neptune.

"Well," said Peggy modestly, "I had a good teacher."

"You could work on a fishing boat like me, if you wanted to," said Neptune.

Peggy felt flattered, but she knew she wasn't meant to be a sea dog like Neptune. "Thanks," she told her friend. "But I belong with my family."

Neptune nodded. "I can tell you love them very much," he said.

Oh, I do, thought Peggy, glancing over at Chloe.

"Who wants ice cream?" asked Dad.

"Me!" cried Chloe, Ruby, and Finn.

Captain Pete and Neptune went home

to bed because they had an early start the next morning, but Peggy and her family drove to the harbor. They stopped outside the Frosty Mermaid and went into the ice cream parlor. There were so many flavors to choose from that it took ages to decide. In the end, Dad got pistachio, Mum got coffee, Ruby got strawberry, and Finn chose one scoop of mint chocolate chip and one scoop of lemon sorbet.

"That sounds disgusting," said Chloe, wrinkling her nose.

"It's the best combination," said Finn, licking his cone.

Chloe ordered a cup of the house special,

which had swirls of pink and purple, blue and green. It was called Mermaid Surprise.

When she had eaten half of it, Chloe set the cup on the ground. "I'm full. You can have the rest, Peggy."

Mmmm! Peggy lapped up the melting ice cream. It tasted delicious!

"I wish we didn't have to go home tomorrow," said Finn, sighing.

"I know," said Ruby, nibbling the end of her cone. "It's so fun here."

"It has been a truly wonderful holiday," said Mum.

Chloe nodded. "I didn't get to see a mermaid," she said. "But thanks to Peggy, I got to see something even cooler—dolphins!"

Peggy's heart swelled with love and pride. She hadn't let her best friend down after all!

"Maybe we'll come here again next summer," said Dad. "What do you think?"

"Yes!" cried the kids.

"Yes!" barked Peggy.

Chloe picked her up, and they all watched the sun setting over the beautiful harbor. Peggy snuggled into her friend's arms and sighed happily. Her first holiday had been amazing, and she couldn't wait to come back!

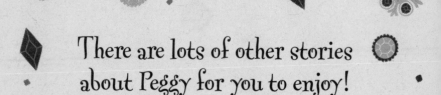

There are lots of other stories
about Peggy for you to enjoy!

THE PUG
Who Wanted to Be
A UNICORN

BELLA SWIFT

THE PUG
Who Wanted to Be
A REINDEER

BELLA SWIFT

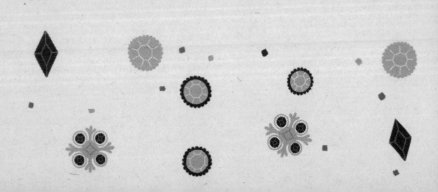

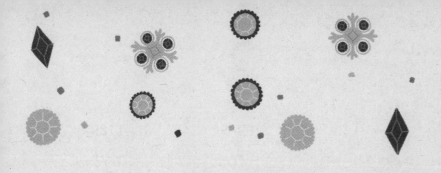

THE PUG
Who Wanted to Be
A BUNNY

BELLA SWIFT

THE PUG
Who Wanted to Be
A PUMPKIN

BELLA SWIFT

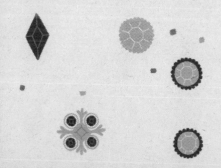

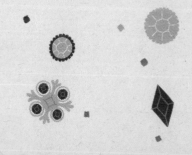

READ&
LEARN
with
simon kids

Keep your child reading, learning, and having fun with Simon Kids!

A one-stop shop where you can
find downloadable resources, watch interactive author videos, browse books by reading level, and more!

Visit us at
SimonandSchusterPublishing.com/ReadandLearn/

And follow us @SimonKids

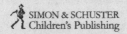 
SIMON & SCHUSTER
Children's Publishing

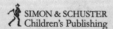